Caroline Patton Hatch

Honour thy father

A sermon in memory of William Weston Patton

Caroline Patton Hatch

Honour thy father
A sermon in memory of William Weston Patton

ISBN/EAN: 9783337196530

Printed in Europe, USA, Canada, Australia, Japan

Cover: Foto ©Andreas Hilbeck / pixelio.de

More available books at **www.hansebooks.com**

HONOUR THY FATHER

✝

A Memorial of

WILLIAM WESTON PATTON

Preface

✠

THE object of Dr. Patton's family in sending this Memorial to his friends is declared in the title. Their desire has been to honor him who counted it a sacred privilege to publish a tribute to his own father and mother when their work was done; and whose entire life was characterized by modesty and self-depreciation to a rare degree, although by his devotion to public interests he was often brought into positions of prominence.

An account of Dr. Patton's public career is given in the sermon with which the Memorial opens. This sermon, with the Appendix, was originally printed separately, at the request of many friends in the Westfield Church who were present when it was delivered. In the Appendix, which thus comes in the middle of the volume, appear the Resolutions of the Faculty of Howard University, presented to Dr. Patton upon his retirement from the presidency. They are so appreciative of this last work of his life, and touched him so deeply by their expressions of personal love, as to merit a place here. The Resolutions of The First Congregational Church of Chicago upon the death of Dr. Patton are also given as describing his work as pastor of the church which was his principal charge, and as editor of the *Advance*. Similar resolutions have been received from The Chicago Congregational Ministers' Union, The Washington Association of

Congregational Ministers, The Washington Conference of Congregational Churches, the Executive Committee of Howard University, and the Trustees of Howard University; and are here gratefully acknowledged, as are also the letters of sympathy from friends which came in such numbers as to make a definite answer in each case impossible.

In order to make the Memorial complete, there has been added a sketch of Dr. Patton's Home Life, which will be appreciated by his friends as a more personal account of his character than was possible in the sermon, and as coming from his eldest daughter, who was with him in the home for a longer period than any of the other children.

The Memorial closes with a sermon from Dr. Patton's own pen on, "How to make the next life seem real." The selection was made not because this is the finest specimen of his work as an author, but because it was in a peculiar degree the outgrowth of his own religious experience and habits of thought in respect to the heavenly world. His manner in its delivery was very impressive, and suggested an intense realization of the truths he was uttering. It was one of the last sermons he wrote, and being so much a part of his own life, it seems a fitting farewell to his friends. Many have spoken of the comfort they received from this one sermon of Dr. Patton. May its publication here help others to a fuller realization of the heavenly life into which he has now entered, no longer to know in part and to prophesy in part, but to know even as he is known.

HONOUR THY FATHER

A Sermon in Memory of

WILLIAM WESTON PATTON

BY HIS SON
REV. CORNELIUS H. PATTON

Congregational Church of Christ
WESTFIELD, N. J.

APRIL 13
MDCCCXC

" I SHALL NEVER THINK MYSELF OLD UNTIL MY WORK IS DONE, AND THAT WORK WILL NOT BE DONE WHILE I KNOW AND WILL WHAT I OUGHT. . . . TO THE END OF LIFE I AM DETERMINED TO GROW STRONGER AND LIVELIER BY EVERY ACT, AND MORE VITAL THROUGH EVERY SELF-IMPROVEMENT. I WILL WED YOUTH TO AGE, SO THAT THE LATTER MAY BE FILLED AND THOROUGHLY PENE-TRATED WITH INSPIRING WARMTH. . . . . . WHEN THE LIGHT OF MY EYES SHALL FADE, AND THE GRAY HAIRS SHALL SPRINKLE MY BLONDE LOCKS, MY SPIRIT SHALL STILL SMILE. NO EVENT SHALL HAVE POWER TO DISTURB MY HEART ; THE PULSE OF MY INNER LIFE SHALL REMAIN FRESH WHILE LIFE ENDURES."—*Schleiermacher*.

Honour Thy Father

EXODUS XX. 12.

✤

SO begins the fifth of the ten great commandments of God. The four that precede relate
to the honoring of God. "I am the Lord thy
God," stands at the head of all these words; and
because of this fact there is enjoined upon us, the
recognition of him as the one true deity, the
upholding of his purely spiritual nature, the according to him of the reverence due his name, and the
rendering unto him of worship at appropriate times
and seasons. Then follows the command for the
honoring of parents. God himself thus honors the
father and the mother in placing their honor next
to his own.

The reason for this is found in the fact that the
relation of parents to their children is analogous to
the relation of God toward his people. It is true,
the parent has a right to honor from his children,
because of what he personally is to them; as
though before the fifth commandment there stood
the words, "I am thy father in the flesh," as there
stands before the first commandment the declara-
tion, "I am the Lord thy God." But in addition
to this, the Bible teaches that in many respects the
parent stands for the child in the place of God; and

so shares in the divine honor. If the commandments were divided between the two tables so that there were five on each (as there is good reason to suppose was the case), then this commandment respecting parents was classed with those commonly described as prescribing man's duty to God. The honoring of parents being grounded in the divine side of their position would thus be taken up into the honoring of God himself. Moreover, the specific regulations of the Levitical law pertaining to the duties of children toward their parents seem to bear out the same idea. The law required that irreverence, or disobedience toward parents, should be punished in the same way as irreverence, or disobedience toward God, viz., by death. And comparing Exodus with Deuteronomy, we find that the promises relating to faithfulness in both of these relations are closely akin.

Since, then, we are called upon to honor our parents for the sake of God, as well as because of what they personally are to us, we can see that there is an especial appropriateness in emphasizing the honor due a father. God has chosen this of all earthly titles to represent his relation to us. He pre-eminently is our Heavenly Father. And we may be sure that this of the many names he bears is the dearest to him, because he has given it to us last, and mainly through the revelation of his only begotten, his well beloved Son, Jesus Christ. There is a peculiar sacredness in the honor which children are permitted to render to their fathers; and if providentially they are born to fathers who are god-like in character as well as in position, who themselves are "sons of God," then blessed indeed is their honoring of them. Upon such an one God enjoins this duty in double measure, requiring of him reverence, obedience and service during life, and a corresponding tribute after his father's death.

With me personally it has seemed that the best tribute I could pay to him who has stood to me in this sacred relation, would be through the endeavor to nourish within myself, and so manifest to the world, all that was noble, great and godly in him. When a man has been of value to the world, the best possible tribute that he can have after death is the reproduction and continuation of his life in others and especially in his children. Such an honoring of a father is a living and abiding memorial ; and so more to be desired than a setting forth in words of what his life has been. And yet there is a place for the verbal tribute. The command to honor thy father includes the recognition of his worth among men by word of mouth, as well as by deed and life. As with that higher relation mirrored in this, in the heart is found the essential honor, but " with the mouth confession is made."

I rejoice that in the providence of God there is granted to me a special opportunity in this way ; and I am sure you all will rejoice to have me use it. In a promiscuous gathering such words as I desire to speak might be deemed inappropriate; but certainly not here. In this little church we are a family; and into our circle, he of whom I shall speak sought to come. As a member of this church, if God was willing, he desired to spend his last days, and every step had been taken toward entering into such a relation to us, except the formal reception on the Lord's Day. But the Heavenly Father planned far better for him, and so in telling you the story of his life, I am but making you acquainted with one whom you expected to know and appreciate by seeing him go in and out among you day after day.

William Weston Patton was born on the 19th of October, 1821. He was the oldest surviving child of Rev. William Patton, D.D., and Mary Weston Patton.* At the time of his birth his father was pastor of the Central Presbyterian Church of New York City. His father was a man of great individuality and power, as several of our own congregation here can testify, having sat under his ministry in their youth. Anecdotes are abundant to-day in these parts of his strength as a preacher, and his rare gift of humor and geniality in conversation. His commanding presence, together with his original way of enforcing the truth, gave his sermons a re-

---

* The other living children of Dr. William Patton are: Mrs. Mary P. Comstock, Hartford, Conn.; Ludlow Patton, New York City; Mrs. Catharine P. Howard, Hartford, Conn.; Mrs. Emily P. Perkins, London, England.

markable staying quality. Few heard him without being impressed, and having the substance of the discourse remain in the mind. "I remember a sermon which your grandfather preached," is a phrase with which I have become very familiar of late years. His ministry was divided principally between the Central Presbyterian Church, which he himself organized in Broome Street, and the Spring Street Presbyterian Church. He also filled the Secretary's chair in the Educational Society, and for a time was pastor of a Congregational Church in Hammond Street. He was the original suggester of both the Union Theological Seminary, and the Evangelical Alliance, and was numbered also among the founders of these institutions. The latter part of his life he spent in the writing of books.

As for the inheritance which came to my father from more remote ancestors, it may be stated that his grandfather, Col. Robert Patton, belonged to a Scotch-Irish family and removed to this country in his youth. He gained his title in the War of the Revolution, where he served under Washington and Lafayette. Afterwards he was appointed the first Postmaster of Philadelphia under the new Government, a position which he held continuously for about thirty years. He was a man of remarkably strict integrity, and of strong anti-slavery views.

And now what shall I say of the mother? She was a good mother, a native of Massachusetts, a Christian from early years, very warm and loving in her disposition, and desiring above all things to have her children followers of the Lord Jesus Christ. She taught my father his letters from the great family Bible, and watched the development of his life as a boy and as a minister with intense interest.

My father at eight years of age was sent to a boarding-school conducted by his uncle at Princeton, N. J., where at once he started upon the study of Latin and Greek along with the common English branches. Four years were spent there, and two more at various schools, his academic education being completed at a private academy in Torringford, Conn. In 1835, when only fourteen years of age, he entered upon his college course at the University of the City of New York. He was naturally a bright scholar, and enjoyed study ; so that he was enabled to stand high in all his classes. But at this period of his life he was noted quite as much for his willfulness and his mischievous qualities as for his attainments in scholarship. He frankly bore testimony in later years to the trouble and worry which he caused his parents and instructors in these years of which we are speaking.

But one day, while he was a student in College, he wrote on the blank page of his Bible the following words : "I hereby resolve to give myself away to the Lord, and separate myself from the world." It was brought about by a trip with his father to New Haven, where some special meetings were being held, attendance upon those meetings, a walk in the fields with a ministerial friend, and by the Holy Spirit. That was March 24, 1837. I mention the exact date because it was the beginning of an entirely new life to my father. The change of heart which he then experienced was absolute. During all the rest of his life he looked back upon that day with peculiar tenderness. And when fifty years had rolled around, and he found himself at the head of a University, he preached to the young men under him, from the text: "Come and hear, all ye that fear God, and I will declare what he hath done, for my soul." He was naturally reticent about relating his own spiritual experience; but under the power of the fiftieth return of that spiritual birthday, he opened his heart, and told the story of his coming to the Lord, and the way God had led him since that time. It was but doing before others, in his desire to win those young men to Christ, what every year he did to himself on his knees before God, when the 24th of March came round. It is noteworthy also, that upon the day of his conversion he began keeping the journal which he continued uninterruptedly throughout his life.

One who knew him as a boy states that he was a leader even then. Among his comrades he never followed. It was always "Come, boys," in playing top and kite and ball. He was the originator and leader in all that they did, and especially in their mischief. But immediately upon conversion all this energy of his nature and his natural ability for leadership were turned into the service of Christ. In the University among his fellow-students, in the Church and in the community he went to work with a zeal that was remarkable. His father, just before this time, had given up the pastorate of the Broome Street Church, and was attending Dr. Skinner's Church, on Mercer Street. It was a delightful place to attend worship in many respects, but my father regarded it as "too wealthy, fashionable and worldly," and as affording small opportunity for doing good. He therefore united with a small Mission Church, and engaged in work there. Later, when his father became pastor of the Spring Street Church, where there was a vast field for Christian energy, he transferred his membership to that body.

About the same time he graduated from college, and entered the Union Theological Seminary of New York City. The idea of becoming a minister of the Gospel came to my father simultaneously with his conversion. He was converted into the ministry as well as into the Christian life. While engaged in his theological studies, which he pursued with great diligence, he was also intensely active in the Church. He formed a large Bible Class of young ladies, whom, according to the custom then, he met twice on Sundays, and visited with great faithfulness during the week, for the sake of personal conversation upon religion, at the same time making each member a special object of prayer. I

have found an old blank-book containing the record
of that class work. One hundred and eleven names
of young ladies are entered ; and when he left them
to enter the ministry, nearly all of them had been
brought to Christ ; and he records the fact that of
all who remained steadily in the class only one
continued obdurate. What a record! And it was to
be made yet more complete; for twenty-seven years
after, on a Sunday morning, at the close of the
service, a lady was waiting for him at the foot of
the pulpit steps. It was the one member of his
class who, notwithstanding his many prayers and
entreaties, had remained out of the fold. After ex-
changing greetings, his first question was, "Har-
riet, do you love the Lord Jesus Christ?" And, to
his unutterable joy, she replied, "Yes, I trust I
do." *

He was also one of the leading spirits in the
prayer meetings of the Spring Street Church, and
especially in the meeting held at six o'clock on Sunday mornings during times of special interest, which
seem to have been nearly all the time in that
church. Week after week he would rise at five
o'clock to open the church and light the fire for
that service. During the same period he was also
a worker for the American Tract Society, oversee-
ing a district in the city, and visiting high and low
within its borders.

To appreciate the energy of his Christian life we

---

* See " Prayer and its Remarkable Answers," p. 307.

need to follow him on one of his vacations. It was to Granville, N. Y., that he went one summer to spend a season of recreation in the country. But having been asked to lead one of the prayer meetings in the little church of the town, he preached Christ so effectively that a revival sprang up at once. The minister seeing that the Lord was using this young man, asked him to take charge of the services, which he consented to do, preaching night after night. The work continued as long as his vacation lasted, and when he went home the people gave him so many evidences of their love that he was quite overcome, and prayed God to be kept humble. And now that I have related this incident thus far, I might as well finish it, although what followed is a curious commentary upon the narrowness of some of the ministers of that day. In the course of time the pastor of the Granville Church reported to the Presbytery the large accession to his church as the result of that summer's work. He stated that a son of Dr. Patton, of New York, had been among them, and his preaching had been greatly blessed.' But when questioned by the ministers, the fact came out that this young evangelist had not been licensed to preach, and immediately the disapprobation of the Presbytery was made manifest. A communication was sent in post haste to the Union Theological Seminary and to the father of the culprit, insisting that such doings were irregular and must be stopped.

They had no further occasion for worry, however, as during the next vacation, to avoid the recurrence of such a disturbance, as well as for his own improvement, it may be assumed, his father started him for England on board a sailing vessel. The voyage was long, and being outside the domain of any ecclesiastical body, he was enabled to preach to the sailors and his fellow passengers to his heart's content. And a year after his return he was examined by the Presbytery of New York, and was approved as a preacher of the Gospel, so far as man was concerned.

He had received his commission from God long before, and so it was with great joy that the next Sunday he entered his father's pulpit to preach his first regular sermon, being twenty years old. The people all wondered to see him there, so youthful was his appearance. His mother, down in the front pew, wept all through the service, and his father behind him was much overcome.

We have reached now, the year 1843. He was married during January of that year to Sarah Jane Mott, of New York City, a young lady from his Bible Class, of rare sweetness of character, and who entered earnestly and sympathetically into his work during the seven years she was spared to him. She became the mother of three of his children, two of whom died during childhood. One week after his marriage he was ordained over the Phillips Congregational Church of South Boston, Mass. They had

waited for him six months, until he was of age, he
having declined to become their pastor before that
time. He became the pastor of a Congregational
Church because of the greater liberty which was
offered to him there as a minister. He found himself out of accord with the Presbyterian ministers
on several points, especially in his strong anti-slavery
opinions, and to avoid the repression which the
Presbyteries at that time exercised in that direction,
he espoused the New England faith, of which he
became an able expounder and enthusiastic advocate.

At his ordination, however, he learned that narrowness was not confined to any one denomination.
Some of the Council objected strongly to the fact that
he had a leaning towards the view of santification
which was advocated by President Mahan of Oberlin,
and Rev. Charles G. Finney. Some of the ministers
insisted that he should pledge himself not to admit
these brethren to his pulpit. This he resolutely
refused to do. The discussion and the examination
over this point were earnest and long ; they were pro-
tracted even into the evening. The hour for the
evening service arrived; and the church was filled
with a waiting and a wondering throng. Finally,
one hour after the appointed time the Council appeared and proceeded with the ordination. Thirty-
one years later Dr. Patton was a delegate at the
meeting of the National Council of Congregational
Churches in Oberlin, Ohio. There he had the grat-

ification of hearing the Council, composed of distinguished clergymen from all parts of the land roused to a high pitch of enthusiasm by an address from Mr. Finney, unanimously request him to preach to them on the following Lord's Day.

It is remarkable how many conspicuous reversals of public and ministerial opinion my father lived to see. From the first he was broad, tolerant, and farsighted. This led him to take positions far in advance of many of his day, and hence to clash with not a few of his brethren of a narrower turn of mind. He held to his opinions manfully and often at the cost of fellowship with other ministers, and even of personal friendships. He did not worry or fret over this, deeply as it grieved him. He trusted that time would work a change ; and how often this proved to be the case ! In fact, the history of his three years at Boston might be summed up as an illustration of this. He was drawn to that field because of the prevalence of the anti-slavery sentiment in the city, and yet he found very soon that many of the prominent men in his own church did not accept his advanced positions on that subject. This with theological differences led some of the older members to remonstrate with him. He appreciated the fact that he was exceedingly young to be the teacher of these men, and so it was a sore trial that in order to be true to himself he had to go contrary to their opinions. He felt this particularly with reference to one of his deacons, who himself a very conscientious and faithful Christian, thought his pastor was making not a few mistakes. Many were the conversations they had together over these vexed points. Personally they were good friends, but when my father left the church to go to another field, he felt that it must be a great relief to good Deacon Drake.

But this is what happened. Some forty years after, when he was a resident of Chicago, Ill., a lady called at his house and related what had recently happened at a meeting in the old Phillips Church, South Boston, when they were discussing the merits of various candidates for the pastorate which was then vacant. They had heard an elderly man, a middle aged man and a young man, and the opinions were various. Most of them, however, inclined toward calling one of the more mature candidates ; when Deacon Drake, now an old man, quietly arose and said : " I have been in this church a good many years and I have known the ministers well. Sometimes we have had pastors who were well along in life and sometimes we have had those who were younger, and once I remember we had a mere boy, and it is my belief that the church never did better than when we had the boy." My father told me that never in his life, had any commendation touched him like that testimony from Deacon Drake. To use his own words, " I nearly fell down, I was so amazed." It was not so much that in the progress of time his old opinions had been justified, but that the mistakes which he felt he had made because of his immaturity had been so generously overlooked, and that in spite of them he had accomplished much good in Boston.

In January, 1846, he accepted a call to the Fourth Congregational Church of Hartford, Conn. The eleven years he spent there were a time of great activity. The church was not strong and the management of nearly all its affairs, financial as well as spiritual, fell upon him. In both spheres he worked with a tireless energy. He soon saw the need of a better church edifice and in a different location, and it was mainly through his personal efforts that a large, fine building was constructed, paid for and then filled. This same building is in use to-day, the Fourth Church occupying a commanding position in the city for the furtherance of city missionary work. It is now manned with two pastors.

The history of the church during the time of my father's pastorate was marked by a succession of revivals. There was a notable increase in the membership of the church, and in the spirituality of the people. The people were a unit with their pastor in his opposition to slavery. The work in this direction to be done at that period was mainly among the churches to bring them to a sense of the evil of slavery and their duty in respect to it. And so from the Fourth Church as head-quarters in Hartford, the agitation was carried into church gatherings and especially into the Annual meetings of the great religious societies, such as the American Board and the American Tract Society. When the American Board refused to forbid slave-holding by the members of their churches in the Indian Territory, the Fourth Church drew up a protest which their pastor presented at the Annual Meeting of the Board. Its effect may be judged from the fact that as soon as its purport was apparent, a leading Corporate Member, the pastor of a church in Washington, D. C., rose up, and shouted at the top of his voice: "Young man sit down. We don't care to hear from you." That was the end of the protest. But it was one of the unique experiences in my father's life, some forty years later when President of a University to educate a free colored race, to conduct the graduating exercises of the Theological Department from the pulpit of that same church whose pastor had so violently opposed that early plea for the slave.

It was also as an opponent of the American Board at this period on the question of slavery. that he became one of the organizers of the American Missionary Association. And in every way by sermons preached and published, by lectures delivered in many places and by editorials in the *Religious Herald*, the denominational paper of the State whose management had been committed to him, he sought to aid the great reform.

Domestic affliction came to him at Hartford, in the death of his wife and two of his children. It was there also that he found his second companion, Mary Boardman Smith, to whom he was married, October 1, 1851. For twenty-nine years they labored together. Through her refined nature, her rich intellectual endowments, and her rare capacity as a mother and as a leader among women, she was enabled to add greatly to his efficiency in the various positions he filled, and to be a strong influence upon his personal character. She became the mother of six children, four sons and two daughters, all of them living to-day.*

While at Hartford he came in contact with two remarkable men who had so much influence upon his after life and thought, that special mention should be made of them. One was Dr. Horace Bushnell, the great theologian, and I may add heretic of his time ; and the other was Mr. Finney the evangelist, whom I have already mentioned. Dr. Bushnell was pastor of the North Church of Hartford when my father was there; and it was during this period that he went through his great controversy with the other ministers of the State His doctrines were regarded as so unsound by many of the ministers that they refused to fellowship with him ; and steps were even taken to depose him from

---

* The surviving children of Dr. Patton are as follows :—By his first marriage ; William L. Patton, New York City. By his second marriage ; Normand S. Patton, Chicago, Ill.; Robert W. Patton, Chicago, Ill.; Mrs. Caroline P. Hatch, wife of Rev. David P. Hatch, Rockland Maine ; Horace B. Patton, Rutgers College, New Brunswick, N. J.; Cornelius H. Patton, Westfield, N. J.; Mrs. Mary P. Welles, wife of Martin Welles, Westfield, N. J.

the ministry. My father while not agreeing entirely with Dr. Bushnell's views, was yet abundantly willing to tolerate them, and being entirely frank in his attitude toward both parties, it happened that he became a sort of go-between for Dr. Bushnell and his chief opponent Dr. Hawes ; and it was quite largely through his instrumentality that a reconciliation was finally effected between these great leaders. This led to a close acquaintance with Dr. Bushnell, a warm friendship, which was kept up until the death of the great theologian, and a large appreciation of his character and ability.

With Mr. Finney the contact was of a still closer kind, but shorter in duration. Mr. Finney stayed at his house during one winter when revival services were being held, and the attachment which had begun before now ripened into a close bond of sympathy, which bore abundant fruit in after life. My father has written this in his journal: "I am more indebted to Mr. Finney than to any other man for theological clearness on many essential points, and for knowing how to preach with reference to immediate effect on the hearer." He considered it a great blessing to have known intimately two such men as Dr. Bushnell and Mr. Finney. They were widely different from each other, but I can see that coming into contact with my father during the formative years of his ministry, they had a powerful influence upon him, and that there was effected a sort of amalgamation of them in his life. As a

preacher and writer he had not a little of the progressive, thoughtful, logical ability of Bushnell, together with the earnest, common-sense, practical
power of Finney. And with them both he hated
narrowness and intolerance, and fought it whenever
it appeared.*

In January, 1857, he was installed over the First
Congregational Church of Chicago, Ill. He was
selected to fill this important position largely
because of his anti-slavery views and practices,
together with his known ability as an organizer
and preacher. The Northwest was just beginning
to enter upon its period of remarkable growth, and
there was a rare opportunity for the progressive
pastor. As standing at the head of the oldest
church of the denomination in the city, he was

---

*The reference to Dr. Patton's indebtedness to Dr. Horace
Bushnell suggests an incident which testifies to the quality of his
sermons, and also to his remarkably playful disposition. Mary
Boardman Smith, who became his second wife, was a member of
Dr. Bushnell's Church and a great admirer of her pastor. Dr. Patton was accordingly somewhat apprehensive as to how she would
enjoy the change of ministers. She very generously relieved him of
all anxiety on that point soon after the wedding, but would frequently ask to be read to from a volume of Dr. Bushnell's sermons.
Occasionally she would break in with some such remark as: "There,
isn't that a fine passage! Now, William, if you could only write
like that!" This happened several times, until one day her enthusiasm rose to a particularly high point, and he was frequently
interrupted with the exclamations: "That's beautiful!" "Isn't
that grand!" culminating finally in the question, "There, William,
why don't you write like that?" Whereupon, hardly able to re-
tain his composure longer, he passed the volume over to her; and
she found to her fond dismay that he had been reading from one of
his own old manuscripts, which he had slyly slipped into the book
before beginning.

called upon to take the lead ; and the strong standing of our denomination to-day in Chicago (where we have some forty-five churches), and indeed in the regions beyond, is due in no small degree to his work at that time. His own church immediately became the centre of large missionary undertakings. They carried on four missions at the same time, the object being to form them into independent churches as fast as possible. As soon as such organization was effected in one field, work was immediately begun somewhere else. This policy accomplished wonders in the way of church extension. Union Park Church, now one of the strongest in our entire denomination, was started under Dr. Patton as a mission. This Church has itself sent out many branches ; these in turn have become Churches, and, following the example of the parent and the grandparent, have of themselves established missions.

For better work in the home field, Dr. Patton's own church was divided into twelve districts each with an overseer, who visited regularly and conducted a meeting in his district at stated intervals. In this way the Church grew rapidly ; and the membership increased during his pastorate of ten years from two hundred and sixty-eight to one thousand and fifty-six.*

---

*These figures are taken from the printed report of the Church Clerk at the Twenty-fifth Anniversary of the Church. Other figures are given in the Memorial from the First Church after Dr. Patton's death. See Appendix III.

During the same period the Chicago Theological Seminary was established, Dr. Patton being one of the organizers and serving as President of its Board of Directors. Much earnest and self-sacrificing work he put into this Seminary, which now leads all our Theological Institutions in the number of its students. At the same time he was doing regular editorial work, was delivering lectures at various places, taking a prominent part in the denominational gatherings, in the extension of the churches into the surrounding region, and working all the time for the abolition of slavery.

And then came the war. He had hoped and worked for a peaceful solution of this great question, but when God ordered otherwise he fell into line and from this time on worked harder than ever for the slave and for his country. At the breaking out of the war he gave notice from his pulpit that the men of the congregation would meet every night for drill in the lecture-room of the Church. Many of his young men stimulated by his words enlisted under the lead of the gallant Major Whittle one of his members, now the well-known evangelist.

Thereafter for four years "war sermons" abounded at the First Church. They constitute now a great pile among Dr. Patton's manuscripts. Their texts and subjects are striking and attest the earnestness and thoughtfulness with which he followed every turn of events. The thought which was uppermost in his mind was the bearing of the war upon the emancipation of the slaves ; and it was with a sad heart that during the early stages of the struggle he noticed the indisposition of the government, the army and the leading politicians, to connect that object with the preservation of the Federal Union.

Upon the organization of the Sanitary Commission of the Northwest, he was elected Vice-President, which became the place of general executive management. In this capacity he made frequent visits to the seat of the war in the West, to inspect the sanitary condition of the camps and hospitals.*

But his grandest work at this time was in connec-

---

* On one of these journeys, while riding on the cars, by way of whiling away the time, he scribbled off on the back of an envelope a " New John Brown Song," in which he sought to express the moral issues of the war in relation to slavery, using the first line and chorus of the orignal version which was just then becoming popular. Four of the new stanzas ran as follows :

I.

Old John Brown's body lies a-moldering in the grave,
While weep the sons of bondage, whom he ventured all to save ;
But though he lost his life in struggling for the slave,
His soul is marching on ! O Glory ! Hallelujah !

II.

John Brown he was a hero, undaunted, true and brave,
And Kansas knew his valor, where he fought, her rights to save,
And now, though the grass grows green above his grave,
His soul is marching on ! O Glory ! Hallelujah !

III.

He captured Harper's Ferry with his nineteen men, so few,
And he frightened " Old Virginny," till she trembled through and
    through ;
They hung him for a traitor, themselves a traitor crew,
But his soul is marching on ! O Glory ! Hallelujah !

tion with the great mass meeting in Chicago, which sent a memorial to President Lincoln, urging him to issue a proclamation freeing the slaves throughout the South. The meeting gathered at his suggestion, the memorial was drawn up by his hand, and he was placed at the head of the Committee to present it to the President. This he did with Dr. Dempster, his associate, arguing the matter with Mr. Lincoln, who talked with them freely for an hour, and bade them good-bye, thanking them for their words and promising to give the matter further thought and to do his duty. The day after their report was published in the papers, many of which made light of their hopes, the preliminary proclamation of emancipation was issued. Mr. Lincoln had had the matter under consideration and so welcomed the interview with the Chicago Committee. Their work was that of confirming a desire which already existed in his own heart. As Secretary Stanton remarked to Mr. Medill of the Chicago *Tribune*, " Tell those Chicago clergymen who waited on the President about the Proclama-

---

IV.

John Brown was John the Baptist of the Christ we are to see—
Christ who of the bondman shall the Liberator be ;
And soon throughout the sunny South the slaves shall all be free,
For his soul is marching on ! O Glory ! Hallelujah !

The entire song was afterward printed in the Chicago *Tribune*, and became wonderfully popular in the Western Army. The " Jubilee Singers " some years after adopted two of the stanzas for their use, thus giving them yet wider currency. Wendell Phillips used to quote the third stanza with great effect at times.

tion of Emancipation that their interview finished the business." *

At the close of the war he spent a year traveling in Europe and the Holy Land; and upon his return in 1867 he resigned the pastorate of his church to take the editorship of the *Advance*, a paper which was started as the organ of the denomination in the Northwest. The name was of his own choosing, and it truly represents the work he did as editor for five years. The paper immediately achieved a reputation for the vigorous and broad treatment of questions of the day which characterized its editorial pages. When the business basis of the *Advance* was changed as a result of the great fire in Chicago, Dr. Patton gave up his position on the paper, and for four years devoted himself to work of a more general nature. Part of this time he was Secretary for the West of the American Missionary Association. This was also the period when he wrote his book entitled *Prayer and Its Remarkable Answers*, which went through twenty editions, and to-day is considered by many as the best exposition of prayer on its doctrinal and experimental sides. During the same years he also delivered lectures before the Oberlin and Chicago Theological Seminaries on Scepticism, as well as contributing frequently to the religious papers and reviews.

* For a full account of this Memorial see Publications of the Maryland Historical Society, "President Lincoln and the Chicago Memorial on Emancipation." Rev. W. W. Patton, D.D., LL.D., 1888.

In 1877 there came from the Trustees of Howard University in Washington, D. C., a call to the presidency of that institution. The work there in educating colored young men and women was in the line of the interests and labors of all his past life; and so although the institution was in a precarious condition through the withdrawal of Government aid, he concluded that God wished him to labor there. He removed to Washington with his family in the fall, and at once threw himself into this new work. As President he had much to do with the financial affairs of the University; and here he showed rare discretion and ability. The confidence of the Government was speedily restored, the debt was paid, and the institution placed on a sound and permanent basis. In all his dealings also with the Faculties of the various departments, Normal, College, Industrial, Medical, Law and Theological, he won the respect and love of all, although he often was obliged to rule contrary to the judgment of many of his associates. The students knew him principally as an instructor in the College and Theological Departments, and as a preacher. Every Sunday afternoon he preached in the Chapel. They were strong, practical, faithful sermons directed to the needs of the young men and women under him. He hid nothing from them in respect to the faults peculiar to their race. He pointed out to them also their strong points; and delighted to open up to their vision the great opportunities of an educated

colored man to-day. Especially were his Baccalau-
reate sermons directed to this end. He dealt with
them like a faithful father. It was his own opinion
that he accomplished as much with the students by
his preaching, as he did by his work in the class room.

Dr. Patton filled so many positions that it is impossible for me to speak definitely of each one ; but
it may be remarked that his work as a teacher was
in no respect behind what he accomplished as a
preacher, an editor, and a business manager.* During these same years he was also deeply interested
in all that was going on in the outside world, and
especially in the Congregational denomination.
He was a frequent writer for the *New Englander
and Yale Review.* He served on the Commission
appointed by the National Council to draw up a
new creed to be recommended to the churches.
He will be remembered by many as an earnest advocate of toleration in the American Board for
those who hold what are known as the Andover
views, although he himself did not take their theological position. To omit any mention of this
would be an injustice to him, so deeply did he feel
on this subject. But having lived to see many
other changes in institutional policies, one notable
change being in the American Board itself, he was
confident that time would set this matter right also.

---

* It was while President of Howard University that Dr. Patton
received from his Alma Mater the degree of LL. D., having received
the degree of D. D. some years before.

Many others will remember him for the delightful sermons he wrote every spring while President of the University, and preached during the summer on his visits North. *

Domestic affliction overtook him again while in Washington, through the death of his wife in the fall of 1880. The loneliness and sorrow which came from this loss, together with the scattering of his children and the increasing cares of the University, which he felt more as his years advanced, led him to resign his position after twelve years of service. His wish was to spend the remainder of the life that God should give him, in comparative retirement, making his home with his two youngest children here in Westfield, and engaging in literary work and in general usefulness as there might be opportunity.

To say farewell to Washington tried him sorely, and those parting occasions with the University and the Church which he had attended partook of such a tender nature as to seem now almost prophetic. The testimonials which came to him from the Trustees and from the Faculty of the University, with

---

* The subjects of these last sermons reveal the wide scope of his mind, his courage, and his progressiveness. They were such as these: "Ease is a sign of power"; "Religious Cant"; "Count Tolstoi and the Sermon on the Mount"; "Alleged Melancholy of the Cultivated Classes"; "The Old and the New"; The Sceptical Argument from the Vastness of the Universe"; Seeming Contradictions in the Divine Character "("God is Love".—"God is a consuming fire".) "Weak Points of the Evangelical Faith, as it is Commonly Stated"; "The Protective Power of Christian Hope"; "How to make the Heavenly Life seem more real."

the remarks which were made at the last prayer meeting of the church were to him overwhelming. As he read one of those testimonials, an exceedingly generous recognition of his work, he exclaimed: "This is almost too much for a poor, imperfect mortal. It describes what I wanted and aimed to be; and I thank God, if my colleagues and friends think that I have made any approximation to so high a standard, while I feel humbled by my knowledge of my own shortcomings." *

You all know the end; the two happy Sundays which he spent with us here, and how the Lord suddenly called him to Himself on the morning of the very day that his connection with Howard University ceased—December 31, 1889.

He was in his sixty-ninth year when he died, not a very old man; and yet his was in a remarkable degree a finished life, so much so, that even the deepest sorrow cannot hide the beauty of the departure. And I think those who have lived nearest to Dr. Patton can testify that his life was finished within, as well as without. For back of all the work he accomplished ,in the various positions he filled, back of it all and grander far was the character of the man. He loved character. He impressed it upon his children: he preached it in his sermons, he exemplified it in his life. Some there are who knowing him in youth and in the

---

* See Appendix II.

ripeness of his last years, appreciate what may seem
strange to many that his life was a spiritual warfare
from beginning to end, and that if toward the close
of life he was possessed of rare symmetry and beauty
of character, it was because lovingly he had sub-
mitted to the educating and refining influences of
his heavenly Father. In no direction perhaps was
this more apparent than in the mellowing and
sweetening of his feelings toward the opinions and
short-comings of others. A strong sense of justice
and righteousness he always had; but more and
more was this tempered with the element of love
and forbearance as life advanced.

He was pre-eminently a man of prayer. His fifty-
three years after conversion were a constant walk
with God, a looking to his Heavenly Father for
guidance at every step in life. Moreover he had an
intensely reverent spirit. He regarded God with
an awe and affection that were inexpressible. It is
not without significance that his prayers in public
almost invariably began with adoration of God for
his majesty, his holiness, and his love; while nothing grieved him more than a light or trivial reference to divine things.

He was a liberal man, giving abundantly of his
substance unto the Lord. He was a remarkably
conscientious man. Those who have ever had a
glimpse into his method of work have been impressed by his systematic quality and his incessant
industry. With all his duties in the various posi-

tions which he held and the distractions of a large family, he yet found time to do an enormous amount of reading and to keep himself informed of what other people were doing in spheres different from his own. He was naturally somewhat reserved in his bearing toward others, but this did not keep from the sight of those who knew him well his really genial and warm nature, while to those closest to him he was simply running over with good cheer and mirth.

No one who knew him well can have failed to notice the extreme simplicity of his life, his modesty and even self-depreciation, and consequent dislike of pushing himself. He who was so energetic in fighting the battles of others, was very slow to urge a claim of his own. The great stands that he has made in public life have not been in the remotest degree from a desire to be prominent, but have been the result of his devotion to the truth, and his entire consecration to duty arising from strong convictions. If he was ever the first upon his feet in a public assembly, and energetic in his opposition to any measure, it was because he literally spake as he was moved. On this account it befell him on not a few occasions to express sentiments which others felt, but dared not utter. And some on this account have thought him naturally severe; but O, how positively his friends can testify that such was not the case! There was no truer or more sympathizing friend of a just cause than he, no kindlier person to go to in trouble.

If there was ever any antagonism in him, it was to men's ideas and not to themselves. It was characteristic of him to notice and call attention to the good qualities of men and their work, especially when others were expressing nothing but blame. And as for those who seemed his bitterest enemies, they all received such loving consideration from him that many came to learn in that way for the first time the rare personal kindliness of his nature. His heart was full of love as his face was radiant with the joy of fellowship with Christ ; and this it was that kept him young to the last day—yes, even to the last hour of his life. He was pushing one of the little girls of our congregation up the hill on her tricycle when the summons came to him from on high. That was the last act of his life ; and his last uttered regret was that he had not been able to push her all the way. Let the record rest with that ; it was typical of what his life had been.

In telling thus simply the story of my father's life I have been obliged to omit much of interest ; but I hope and pray that what has been told will lead some here to greater consecration to the Master, and draw others into the blessed service in which his life was spent.

APPENDIX

A FEW additional details in regard to the death of Dr. Patton and an account of the funeral service will be of interest to his friends. Dr. Patton apparently was in the best of health until within a few hours of his death. He was with his son, Rev. C. H. Patton, on Monday afternoon, Dec. 30th, and walked briskly with him to the post-office, where they parted. He then started for the house of his daughter, Mrs. Martin Welles. On the way he was helping a little girl on a tricycle up a hill when he was taken with shortness of breath. He continued a short distance with difficulty, but finally was obliged to call to a passing carriage to take him home. After reaching his daughter's house he rallied and conversed freely. He was in no pain. At nine o'clock in the evening he was carried upstairs, and at ten o'clock was resting quietly, except for labored breathing and occasional coughing; but at midnight he grew worse rapidly. Severe congestion of the lungs set in and deprived him of breath at one o'clock. He was conscious to the end.

The funeral service was held in the Congregational Church in Westfield, N. J., on the afternoon of January 3, 1890. Dr. Patton's five sons and a nephew bore the body into the church, which had been trimmed with flowers by the young ladies of the parish. The church was filled with the relatives and friends of Dr. Patton, who came together to thank God for all that his life had been to them and to the world.   Rev. S. M. Newman, D.D., his pastor, who conducted the service, spoke particularly of the unabated youthfulness of Dr. Patton, and of his success in carrying over into each period of his life all that was best and most characteristic of the periods coming before.

Rev. W. H. Ward, D.D., of the *Independent*, a friend of many years' standing, alluded to the important work of Dr. Patton as Pastor, Editor, and College President, and dwelt particularly upon his progressiveness, the breadth and liberality of his character.   Rev. M. E. Strieby, D.D., told of his own intimate relations to Dr. Patton in connection with the American Missionary Association, characterizing his work for the Negro race as the chief feature of his life.   The service closed with a song of triumph, Dr. Patton's favorite hymn:

> " Ten thousand times ten thousand,
>   In sparkling raiment bright,
> The armies of the ransomed saints
>   Throng up the steeps of light :
> 'Tis finished, all is finished,
>   Their fight with death and sin :
> Fling open wide the golden gates,
>   And let the victors in."

On the following day the remains were conveyed to Hartford, Conn., and deposited in the Spring Grove Cemetery, by the side of those of his two wives and his two children, who had died in infancy. The prayer at the grave was by Rev. J. H. Twichell, of Hartford.

II

Testimonial from the Faculty of the College and Preparatory Departments of Howard University.

Rev. Wm. W. Patton, D.D., LL.D., having severed his connection with Howard University, and being now about to retire from immediate participation in its concerns as President, the Faculty of the College and the Preparatory Departments desire, at this time, to put on record an expression of its appreciation of the retiring Executive and of the circumstances attending his departure from the University.

We have always found in Dr. Patton, a man of exalted excellence of personal character, of broad and liberal mind, of high and varied culture, of considerate, clear and generous judgment, of great considerateness and sympathy, and of singular aptness for the important work he was called to do. In him also we have found, upon occasion, an appreciative friend and adviser, and it is with a sense of personal bereavement, that we are compelled to consent to a severance of the existing relationship.

For more than twelve years Dr. Patton has been the administrative head of the University, presiding in the councils of the Board of Trustees and participating actively in the instruction of classes in the Theological and the College Departments. By his able management he has shaped and administered a policy which, from a condition of affairs that might well have been considered alarming and desperate, the University has arisen to an extent unexampled in its previous history, to a position of eminence and power in the community and in the country at large, gratifying to all its friends and full of hope for the future. Within and without, so far as known, essential harmony and hopefulness everywhere prevails.

At the age of nearly seventy years, after a long public life as preacher, editor, teacher, and University President, Dr. Patton, looking out from the sunshine of vanishing years, over a checkered and useful life, is permitted to see many good works done for the benefit of humanity, and, not the least of them, the upbuilding and enlargement of Howard University. We congratulate him upon the successful outcome of his busy life, and as he voluntarily lays down active, official duties, and betakes himself to the enjoyment of well-earned leisure among his children and friends, we invoke upon him the blessings of Heaven.

III.

First Congregational Church
OF CHICAGO

Tribute to the memory of
REV. WILLIAM WESTON PATTON, D.D.

PASTOR OF THE CHURCH
FROM JANUARY 8, 1857 TO JULY 16, 1867

ADOPTED JANUARY FIFTH
MDCCCXC

To the First Congregational Church and Society :

Y OUR Committee appointed to prepare a statement and resolution on the death of Rev. William W. Patton, D.D., LL.D., would submit the following report :

The REV. WILLIAM WESTON PATTON, D.D., LL.D., was born in New York City, Oct. 19, 1821, his father being an eminent minister of the Gospel. He graduated at the University of the City of New York, in 1839, and at Union Theological Seminary, New York, in 1842. He became Pastor of Phillips Congregational Church, Boston, Mass., in 1843, and of the Fourth Church, Hartford, Conn., in 1846. In 1857 he came to Chicago to take the pastoral oversight of this church and society. He was already known as a fearless friend of liberty, and his well-known position on the question of slavery made him especially acceptable to this Church. As pastor of this Church, Dr. Patton soon acquired a national reputation as a champion of the rights of the slave, and as the clouds gathered over the Republic, and finally the storm burst in the terrors of Civil war, he was among the first to see and say that the Freedom of the Slaves should be the first fruits of the Harvest of Death. He took a leading part in bringing about President Lincoln's Proclamation of Emancipation. During the war for liberty he was Vice-President of the Northwestern Sanitary Commission, and in its healing service visited the Eastern and Western armies ; he used his pen also vigorously in the service of the suffering soldier and the slave. When the cruel war was over, Dr. Patton continued his deep interest in the negro, now emancipated from one bondage, but ready to fall in his helplessness into another ; to pro-

mote the cause of the Freedmen he visited Europe in
1866. His broad humanitarian sympathies ever led him
into the wide field of national movements ; hence it
seemed quite in harmony with his life work that he
should become editor of the *Advance* in 1867, a Congregational paper, founded in Chicago to advocate throughout the Northwest those principles of Christian freedom
and brotherhood so dear to his heart. In 1877, Dr. Patton took another step most natural for him, the life-long
advocate of the enslaved African ; he became President
of Howard University, an institution of learning founded
in the national capital for the higher education of the negro in science and letters, in medicine, law and theology.
Here he labored till the end of the year 1889. He had
just resigned his position ; his successor was ready to
take up the work ; the time for rest had come, a double
rest, and on the last day of the year, the sad news came
that Dr. Patton had died very unexpectedly at the home
of one of his children, of congestion of the lungs.

In this brief statement of the activity of our former
Pastor, we have put in the foremost place his efforts in
behalf of liberty ; we have done so because that seemed
to give the key-note to his character. But Dr. Patton was
a man of wide sympathies, and as Pastor of this Church he
exercised a far-reaching influence in every direction. He
built up this Church in numbers and character. During
the eleven years of his pastorate the membership increased from one-hundred and ninety-eight to
five-hundred and forty-two. He was a fearless preacher of righteousness, temperance, and judgment to come.
He declared the whole counsel of God as he found it in the
Scriptures. He was a clear and instructive preacher, out-

spoken in behalf of what he considered right, loyal to his Church, but no time-server, no servant of expediency. Such a man commanded the respect of his own congregation, won and retained the confidence of his brethren, so that he was soon regarded as the leading minister of our denomination in the Northwest; and was held in honor among all the churches. He soon saw the great importance of a well-educated ministry for the West, and at once took a deep interest in the Chicago Theological Seminary. For eighteen years, 1859 to 1877, he was a leading and influential member of its Board of Directors and its Executive Committee. He gave a course of lectures in the Seminary on Modern Infidelity, during the years 1874 and 1875. He showed his interest in the Institution also by a gift of $1,000, the proceeds of which are to be used for binding books and pamphlets.

Dr. Patton also exerted a wide influence by his writings. His first work was addressed to young men, for whom he always cherished a warm affection. But his most successful book was that on *Prayer, and Its Remarkable Answers.* Here is the source of power and strength in which he ever sought by precept and example to lead his people. Some of the answers to prayer recorded by him were given to him by members of this Church, and the testimony of their hearts to the blessed help of God in time of need was a great joy to the Pastor as he heard such things in his visits from house to house.

He was a man of freedom, of broad Christian charity, a true patriot, a lover of education, a strong preacher, a faithful pastor, a wise counsellor, a friend indeed of all that were laboring and heavy laden. In view of these things, which the older members of this Church know from experience of Dr. Patton as Pastor, and which all have heard of as part of the history of this church, therefore be it

Resolved. 1. That this Church having heard of the recent death of Rev. Dr. Patton, formerly their Pastor, do hereby express their deep estimate of him as a Minister of the Gospel, and a man of blameless life and great Christian activity.

2. That we express to his family our sincere and hearty sympathy with them in their bereavement, with the sure hope that the God of all comfort will make this affliction also work together with all His dealings for their good.

3. That the clerk of the Church be instructed to spread this statement and these resolutions upon the Records of this Church, and to send a copy of the same to each of Dr. Patton's children and to the *Advance.*

> EDWARD P. GOODWIN,
> WM. W. FARWELL,
> GEORGE N. BOARDMAN,
> JAMES H. PEARSON.

Adopted by vote of the Church, Sabbath, January 5, 1890.

Attest :

> THEO. F. BLISS, *Clerk.*

The Home Life of Dr. Patton

"YOU are indeed to be congratulated upon the life and memory of such a father. It was an honor to have known him, how much more to have borne his name, and been one of his household. We never really knew your father until he came to stay with us a little time, and, though it was but for a couple of months, we both grew to love him dearly."

This extract from the letter of a friend gives expression to thoughts shared by others who have come into more intimate relations with our dear father, and we, his children, feel that even this simple memorial of him would be incomplete without more particular reference to his private life than could appropriately be made in the preceding sermon. It thus seems fitting to add a few pages for the purpose of rounding out this other, but no less important side of a well balanced life.

It is surely not a light thing that a man, honored for his wide usefulness and powerful influence in public life, should be equally loved and respected in his own household. At home our father belonged to us. He was naturally domestic in his tastes, and was never happier than when quietly with his family. To the casual acquaintance he might seem distant; to the opponent in a controversy he might seem severe; but to us he was always the same bright companion, with whom we were allowed the greatest familiarity. He was fond of witticisms, small jokes, rhyming jingles, and nicknames, and a deal of passing nonsense, and was also quite ready to enjoy the fun when it happened to be at his own expense, turning off such a hit with a characteristic "hm, hm," of appreciation, and a puckering of his already small eyes, that meant more than a hearty laugh in those of the jovial build. This sense of grim humor at his own predicament often served to carry him through difficulties which might otherwise have weighed him to the ground. It led him to make the best of everything, as for instance in trivial matters, such as forgetting to mail a letter, he would often say, " Now I shall punish myself by going clear back to do it," in such happy ways ignoring anything like impatience. He seemed always to be the same, no matter what happened, and was a thorough disbeliever in moodiness. We never had to wait for him to be in a good humor to grant a request, nor was he put out by interruptions, and there never was a better man to do errands.

Of him as a husband I can only say that he and our mother were truly one, and I do not remember ever to have heard an unpleasant word of difference between them. Nothing will show this better than the following letter written about a month before our mother's death :

"WASHINGTON, D. C., Oct. 1, 1880.
MY DEAR WIFE:
It is twenty-nine years to-day since I first had the right to

call you by this precious title. The time sounds long, but yet seems very short to look back upon. And this shortness is due largely to the pleasantness of the experience during these years; and that again is due to you. What a comfort and a blessing you have been to me, and what a rallying-centre in the household for all the children! Surely you are one of the most popular of mothers, as well as one of the best of wives, and so the unanimous vote of the family has long been, that you were the "Dear Woman." It is occasion for regret that our wedding anniversary of late years so often finds us separated, and that this year it for the first time finds you an invalid. But we will be grateful to God for His many and long-continued mercies, and we will have faith that He will order well our future lot, and spare us to each other and to our children for many happy days to come. With His blessing all will be right.
Your loving husband,
WM. W. PATTON."

The secret of our happy home lies in that last sentence. The underlying thought there was the acknowledgment of God's blessings and the desire to live worthily of their continuance. Religion was not a theory simply, but was carried into the smallest details of life. The children might push their fun to the highest degree of noise and confusion, and nothing would be said; but one word of irreverence brought such a reproof from Father, that we could never forget it, or wish to have it repeated. The early morning hours were never so busy or hurried as to omit the family worship, and at that time the special needs of each day were brought to the Lord; the school duties of the children, any trying experience that lay before some one of the amily, the journey of a departing member were particularly mentioned, so that there was made upon us all an impression of personal responsibility to God. Among our sweetest memories are the Sunday evenings, which always found us singing, and which closed with prayer by each member of the family in turn. In later years, when distance from church prevented attendance in the evening, Father always read aloud from some recent work bearing on the religious topics of the day. These readings were also counted a privilege by friends who not infrequently joined us in this Sabbath hour, and who valued the discussions which often followed.

The second subject of importance which our father instilled into our minds was that, next to Christianity, education was the highest thing to be sought. He often gave, as an explanation why we could not have all we wished, that we must wait until he had finished educating his children before other things could have their place.

Father was a man of incessant activity; he never spoke of being busy or overworked, never mentioned his need of a vacation, but was always occupied. Every moment was turned to account; all the odd ones being devoted to reading. While others were sitting about, waiting for a meal or a carriage, he had quietly pulled out a paper or book and was reading. His daughters would often demur at his doing this while waiting for a concert to begin, but he only smiled and kept right on. Of course this constant application enabled him to master a vast amount of literature, and all branches seemed to possess nearly equal interest. He had a large library, and I once asked him if he had read every book in it, and, with the exception of the encyclopædias, he said he had. Indeed it almost seemed that he had no need of encyclopædias, for his fund of knowledge on all subjects appeared almost inexhaustible. A graduate of Howard University says, "I often went to Dr. Patton with questions which others failed to answer satisfactorily, and not only received an immediate and full answer, but it seemed as if he were waiting for that particular question to be asked."

He never appeared to read poetry, and yet he knew well where to find almost any quotation. He was very fond of a story, and in reading aloud, would be deeply moved by a touching incident, and pause to gain his composure; or he would enter into the love scenes with great zest. A moment later the novel would be laid aside and we would find him deep in theology. The articles on birds in the various magazines always had a fascination for him. Something of a scientist too, he was often referring to books on geology, biology, etc. He had collected quite an interesting cabinet in this line.

But if there was not a book at hand Father could always find something else to do. Once when taking a trip in the White Mountains, while the coach waited for a change of horses, he had tied a bent pin to a string (he was never without a bunch of it in his pocket), had scratched up a worm somewhere, and had caught a trout in a road-side brook.

Fishing was his delight, and he took into his plans, from year to year, the brooks and the very stones where he expected to find the best trout. On one of his expeditions up a brook in the Adirondacks, night overtook him while crossing from one trail to another. He carefully felt his way in the gathering darkness, until further progress was impossible, and then selected a large tree as his resting-place until dawn. The inevitable newspaper was with him, and this time served for a protection, buttoned over his chest. When quite stiff with cold, he went through a vigorous course of gymnastics or counted a few steps from the tree, returning to it after each trip. He often described his sensations afterwards, and how he lay wondering what his children would say if they knew he was spending the night alone in the forest.

His last adventure of the kind, I judge, had been when, as a boy at boarding-school, he ran away and tried to walk home, but was not sorry to be picked up late in the evening by his teacher, who found him shivering in a ditch. That may have been the beginning of his pedestrian trips, which did not always have so untimely an end. I do not doubt that his abundant health and spirits were due to his walking whenever it was possible. He averaged several miles a day, almost never riding, and was certainly one person for whom the "City of Magnificent Distances" had no weariness. His light elastic step was noticeable to everyone, and one of the professors used to say to him, that he was the youngest member of the Faculty, judging from the way in which he could outwalk them all.

Our little cottage in Lake Geneva, Wisconsin, which we occupied for twelve summers, was a blessing to the whole family, and afforded opportunities for the out-door exercise which Father so enjoyed. Sailing, rowing, fishing, bathing, hunting, and, for one or two winters, skating filled many hours of this country life, and were woven into editorials written from the "Editor's Easy Chair" which occupied a window overlooking the beautiful lake, with its ever-changing lights and shadows. Upon one occasion he nearly ended his life in the waters of this lake by the capsizing of a yacht, but after clinging to the boat for some time, the party was rescued, and father found the brisk walk of three miles home sufficient to save him from any ill effects.

There was no one in the family who could write so good a letter as Father. His four pages of fine distinct writing had packed into them every little event of interest, and bits of every-day news that few men would think of, or take the trouble to write; and those who received from him letters of sympathy at the death of a wife or child found that he had a wealth of tenderness and fellow-feeling that brought them unusual comfort.

I may add that Father's correspondence, like his other duties, was never behindhand ; indeed, promptness was in the very fibre of his nature. His accounts always balanced before he left them, and upon the last day of the year we often rallied him upon sitting up all night to find the missing cent. To those who knew this characteristic, it was not the least of the coincidences of his death that he had just finished making up his books for the year, and summarizing his annual expenses, before leaving the house for the last time.

This method was also carried into his benevolence. He considered that to give systematically, and from principle, was the only true way. In 1866, when he went abroad, he left with the church Treasurer drafts upon the Trustees for the monthly collections as they came in order; which is an illustration of his careful planning to meet such obligations before all others. Accurate, business-like, methodical, conscientious, he was a man of truth, a man to trust, and if his friends missed in him a certain suavity of manner which some men possess, they certainly learned to value a commendation from one who would never give it unless deserved.

Our eldest brother speaks as follows, adding an incident which ante-dates my memory : " Father's unwavering adherence to principle all through his public and private life, tempered by justice and consideration for others, particularly after the first few years of his public life, was one of the most marked of his many fine qualities. Just one incident will show his charity for others, when principle compelled a different course of action for himself. Between 1857 and 1860, when the horse cars were first introduced in Chicago, a public meeting was called in Bryan Hall by the religious people of the City, to protest against their use on Sunday. After nearly all the ministers in the City had spoken against Sunday travel, father, at the very end of the evening, and the last one to speak, rose, and in a very quiet way said, that perhaps the meeting had been somewhat hastily called ; and suggested that some of those present might find after a little experience with Sunday travel, that all would not use the cars for the beer garden or purposes of pleasure, but that a large number might use them for attending church. He accordingly moved that the meeting adjourn without action, subject to the call of the chair, and await results, lest they might be a laughingstock to the non-church-going community, and accomplish no good by too-hurried action. At the same time he predicted that the majority of those present, ministers included, would all be riding in the cars on Sunday. Suffice it to say the chairman never called the second meeting.

Twenty years after, I was in Chicago and went to the South Side to hear Father preach. I with a

friend joined him after service, and returned with
him to the West Side. We proposed taking the
cars as the distance was long. His reply was, 'As
long as my health is good I prefer walking to taking the car on Sunday.' He then told me that he
had never ridden in a car on Sunday, and referring
to the meeting in Bryan Hall, at which I was present, added that as far as he knew, although he was
the only minister who did not oppose Sunday cars, he
was the only one of them who had not used them
on Sunday. Ever after this he kept to his principle,
although he never objected to put Mother or any
other lady in the car when she was unable to walk
the distance. This same justice was always exercised toward his children without partiality."

With children Father was kind and entertaining,
and always showed great friendliness to the young
visitors at our house, ever ready with some jocose
word of welcome for his favorites. In his letters
he often inquired for "My friend, Miss ——," or,
"My charming young friend, M."

Father's love for animals was marked. His best
stories to us, when we were children, were about
his pet squirrels which he owned when a boy. He
was always on the best of terms with the family cat,
which always sat upon his knee while he read ; and
his attachment to a canary was really touching.
By patient training he taught the little thing to
know him, and every noon, when lunch was served,
Father's words, "You roguey Dickey," with a shake

of his finger, would send the bird into a flutter of excitement to have the cage door opened ; and after lunch a grand chase was kept up, and enjoyed by both, till Dick allowed himself to be caught and caressed. A tree-toad was the object of his care at another time, and as for the circus, well—the menagerie would take him a long distance when other attractions failed.

These are small matters to mention, but they go to show the naturalness and simplicity of a man whom many thought austere. He was so modest in speaking of himself even to his own family, that we were often in danger of underrating his character and ability, and have often needed others to tell us of his successes.

He was so young in his feelings that it was hard for him to accept the fact of advancing years, and especially the changes of the last year were deeply felt. Two weeks before his death he wrote to a sister-in-law: "It is a curious feeling to have, that one is about to complete his allotted life work; that not much remains for future ambition or labor; that memory is to take the place of hope; that one's interest is to be not in personal affairs, but in the affairs of one's children and grand-children. This would be sad indeed were it the whole case. But the eye of faith can still look forward, and see new openings in the eternal future, whither so many have preceded us, and where we believe, that they are busily and nobly at work."

The last days at the University were full of appreciation of the expressions of kind regard from his friends, and of pain at the laying aside of his beloved work. His letters spoke of its being almost too much for him to bear alone, with no loving wife by his side, as in former changes. One of the last nights, as he left the grounds, there was a remarkable sunset. The friend before referred to, writes: "He fairly awed us at the dinner-table by describing the beautiful sunset he had just witnessed from The Hill, and then adding, 'Just so the sun of my official life is going down; everything is peaceful and serene, I pass over everything in good order to my successor, but *I* am leaving.'"

And thus it was, with a fuller meaning than he knew, upon the last day of his official life his sun went down.

CAROLINE PATTON HATCH.

How to make the next life seem real

✠

" But if we hope for that we see not, then do we with patience wait for it."—ROMANS VIII. 25.

PATIENCE under earthly trials becomes rational and easy, when faith in the eternal future is clear, and hope of immortality is buoyant. But with many it is difficult to make the next life seem real, so that the hope of it shall exert potent influence upon thought and conduct. How shall we become impressed by the unseen? How feel "the power of the world to come"? Allow me to offer a few practical suggestions, my Christian hearers, which may aid you in making the next world appear real.

1.—As a necessary pre-requisite to everything else, *You must keep your heart and life pure.* Nothing so obscures the eternal future as sin, which is the practical denial of it. Sin surrounds the soul with an impenetrable mist. It begets doubt of every spiritual reality, from the fact of the next life, even up to the being of God himself; turning the mind earthward in its vision, in its affections and in its pursuits, till reality seems to attach only to material objects, and hope to be warranted only as to temporal results. Ah! there was fullness of meaning in the beatitude of Jesus:

" Blessed are the pure in heart ; for they shall see God." The vision begins in this life. Purity so develops and exalts the spiritual side of our nature, that all objects to which it is directly related, stand out as real. It thus easily discerns God, as the embodiment of life ; as the fullness of being ; as the supreme reality in the universe ; as the perpetual presence of power, wisdom and love ; as the infinite Person ; as the Heavenly Father. That there should be a coming life, superior to the present, in which the now unseen God shall be better known, and this child soul shall have a blessed vision of the Father's glory, is a self-evident truth to the pure in heart. To doubt it would be to doubt one's own existence.

2.—*We shall be aided in a realization of the next life by thinking of it as a necessary development of the germs, and as a contrast to the limitations and evils of this present life.* We learn many things ideally and we also gain the sense of their reality, by the law of development and contrast. A germ suggests coming growth and final fruit ; by contrast pain suggests pleasure ; ignorance, knowledge ; deformity, beauty ; limitations, expansion ; weariness, rest ; sin, purity. Have we an experience in this life of unripe results, unfinished beginnings, varied and most sorrowful evils? A healthful mind does not, on account of it, sink into pessimism, but simply says : " Yes, this is part of the reality, and it is sad, but the remainder of the reality is equally sure to come, or the universe has lost its balance, and God is no longer God.

We can say with the poet, Helen Marion Burnside:

"O toil and woe, O love and death !
At least we know ye are not all :
Life but begins with passing breath,
Fruition lies beyond the goal."

Every instance of evil should assure you, my hearer, of the certainty of the coming good. A world of beginnings and half-achieved successes, of burdens and cares, of disorder and oppression, of pain and anguish, of weakness and ignorance, of disease and death, of deformity and sin, is like all first stages of existence, a prophecy as well as a present fact :—a prophecy of a second stage of consummation, rest, comfort, order, justice, strength, knowledge, health, life, beauty and holiness. The law of necessary contrast makes the moral darkness suggest the certain approach of light ; as when the black midnight reminds us of the coming glories of the sunrise. And, similarly, our limitations in the experience of good also lead on our hopes to larger realizations.

As this is the suggestion of nature and of reason, so is it everywhere the teaching and practical influence of the Scriptures. " We are saved in hope," says the apostle in the context, and in another place : " Now we see through a glass darkly; but then face to face: now I know in part; but then shall I know even as also I am known." Think of this law of development and contrast, my Christian brother, in hours when you are tempted to make too little of but partial success, or too much of present evils and limitations. "We walk by faith, not by sight." Reality does not depend upon present vision, but upon the laws of the system of which we are part; upon the unalterable appointment of God and the indestructible nature of things. Yet something of vision attends beginnings. By the discerning eye the fruit is seen in the bud. What we now know of God is assurance of fuller knowledge hereafter. Your earthly experience of Christ is earnest, not only of what you are yet to learn of him, but also of the reality of what has become the experience of those who are "absent from the body, and present with the Lord." This incipient stage points on to the promised consummation, when " we shall be like him, for we shall see him as he is." It is not more certain that the present is rooted in the past, than it is that the future is rooted in the present, as regards its developments and its victories. And this because God includes both, and pervades and enbosoms our entire being as immortals.

"Oh, the little birds sang east, and the little birds sang west,
And I smiled to think God's greatness flowed around our incompleteness,
Round our restlessness his rest."
Mrs. Browning.

3.—*You must think much of your personal relation to the next life.* General ideas are apt to be dim and vague. They gain distinctness and vividness, when applied to particular cases, and to personal experience. It is one thing for us to know that there is a continent of Europe, to which thousands resort for business and pleasure; and it is quite another to purchase a ticket, and to make arrangements for the first time to take a steamer to Liverpool or Havre. The moment this is done, Europe becomes a very definite continent, and is for us newly discovered, and replete with interest. And similarly we are not much affected by the general truth, that there is a next world; or by the connected fact, that millions of men are passing thither; or by the well-known certainty that all men will make the transition by death. Therefore, my hearer, reduce it to a particular and personal form. Say often to yourself, yea, carry the thought habitually in mind, that there is another world to which *you* are shortly going, possibly even in a few days. Make the idea pleasantly familiar that soon *your* permanent home will be in the invisible land. Avoid saying to yourself, "Men are mortal," and say, "*I* am mortal." Do not content yourself with remarking, when you see a consumptive near his end, that "our friend A. will not long be with us," but every day remind yourself that your own hour of leaving is fixed, as Paul did, when he said, "The time of my departure is at hand." Keep up this personal anticipation, as you would any contemplated earthly journey, and the heavenly world, thus habitually considered as the approaching home will become delightfully real to your apprehension.

4.—*Make large use of the imagination;* picture to yourself the next life. The importance of the imagination as a faculty of the mind is underestimated in every department of thought and action. It is supposed to afford amusement only, as when we read a popular "work of fiction," and to be related chiefly to the unreal, as when we call something "imaginary"; whereas, its exercise is part of mental education and growth; is a chief inspiration to effort, in every sphere of life; is that which gives us hold of all future realities, earthly or heavenly; and is the source which supplies a large part of our highest enjoyment. Our ideals of life are what regulate our ambitions and our efforts. We are inspired to produce what we have first conceived in imagination. The picture is in the artist's mind before it is on the canvas. The statue stands out in thought before it takes form in bronze or marble. We sometimes ridicule "castles in the air," but no man ever accomplished much who had no night-visions and day-dreams of his coming future. To hope for anything and not to picture it; how can that be possible? To hope for it, and to make it live constantly in the imagination; how can that fail to give it pleasing reality?

The Bible applies this principle to our relation to the next world. It bids us conceive of a definite something set before us, for which we are to strive, as the

ancient runner in the Grecian games did for the expected garland that was now at the goal to be
placed upon his brow. "Forgetting those things
which are behind, and reaching forth unto those
things which are before," said Paul, "I press toward the mark for the prize of the high calling of
God in Christ Jesus." But could he do this without a glowing imagination? Did he not picture to
himself "the glory which should follow" the labors
and sufferings of this present life? Surely he did,
and we too must take the truth about the next life
out of abstract ideas and put it into pictorial im-
ages. We shall no doubt be crude in the artistic
result; but any result that shall give influential
form to the truth is of value. This is not only a
necessity of our nature, but is clearly warranted by
the methods of inspiration. For the Bible pictures
heaven to the imagination, as well as asserts its existence. We are not, indeed, to insist upon a literal
interpretation of the quite variant descriptions
given, now of a temple and then of a city, now of
a feast and then of a worshiping assembly, now of
calm rest, then of rapturous pleasures, and again of
noble activities ; but we are to accept of these im-
ages for present use, to their fullest extent. Eliza-
beth Stuart Phelps was right in her criticised "Gates
Ajar," in this respect—right philosophically and
Scripturally. There are future realities which have
a substantial correspondence, of some kind, to these
representations set before our imagination ; and

God wishes us to gain instruction, inspiration and comfort from these earthly analogies and prophetic symbols.

Be not afraid then, to visit, in thought, the New Jerusalem, the holy city, to pass thro' its gates of pearl, to traverse its golden streets, to walk daily on the banks of the heavenly river, to partake of the fruit of the tree of life, to listen to the song of the redeemed, to gaze on the glory of Him who sitteth upon the throne and on the Lamb. You will thus grow familiar with the place and its inhabitants, and will come to a habitual sense of the thorough reality of the coming life. The eye of faith, aided by the glass of holy imagination, will be so clear that you will seem to gaze as in open, present vision, until your soul is on fire, with eager desire to dwell therein.

> " Thy walls are made of precious stone ;
> Thy bulwarks diamond square ;
> Thy gates are all of orient pearl :
> O God ! if I were there ! "

5.—*Accustom yourself to think of a transition to the next life as perfectly natural,* when viewed in its higher relations. We start back from death as from something unnatural. And such it is, in its outward material aspect, in its lower relations, in those evil accompaniments due to sin. For plainly it puts an end to earthly activity ; it destroys the bodily organization ; it substitutes foul and unsightly corruption for the attractions of beauty ; it removes from sight those whom we love, and they leave no trace of continued being. But these are only part of the facts. They are as the skin and shell of the worm left behind after the beauteous butterfly has taken his flight. The worm might count it unnatural to be withdrawn from its repasts on leaves and from its accustomed paths along the twigs and branches; but to the naturalist precisely the opposite is seen to be true. He, taking in the entire range of the creature's being, declares that it is simply natural for the creeping worm to disappear forever from the plant, and in quite another sphere, in the regions of air, to become the winged butterfly. Similarly, a scientific angel (and such angels there are) writing the natural history of man for the instruction of some other race, might state that first he is born into the planet Earth, and there has an initial stage of growth, but that after a few years he lays aside his earthly body and passes to the higher stage of spirit existence.

The Bible tries to familiarize us with this true conception of our nature, and to teach us that Christ has redeemed our whole being, soul and body, so that the apparent ravages of death are more than compensated in the glories of the resurrection state. Cultivate then the habitual thought that, as on earth your infancy passed into youth, and your youth into manhood, so this mortal form of existence naturally conducts to the immortal form; that as you were born into this life, so you must be born into the next life; and that what we call death here, they call birth in the heavenly world. The poet Rosetti, in his exquisite production of imagination, "The Blessed Damosel," pictures five companions of the virgin Mary, of whom he says:

> " Circlewise sit they, with bound locks
> And foreheads garlanded,
> Into the fine cloth, white, like flame,
> Weaving the golden thread
> To fashion birth robes for them
> Who are just born, being dead."

This view of your relation to the future, if cherished continually, will give great definiteness and reality to the coming life.

6.—*Give its due weight to the superiority in numbers of those who have already made the transition to the next life*, and to the fact suggested by this vastness of number. It is a very literal truth, we utter sometimes, on the death of a man, when we say that " he has joined the majority." Yes, appearances deceive us. We look around us, where we dwell, we travel in foreign lands, we read the census returns of various countries, we notice the computation of geographers that the population of the world is one billion five hundred millions, and earth seems full. The human race appears to be here; to be at home on this planet. And so, when men die, one by one, they seem to be solitary exceptions, sadly leaving the human family and its habitation. But not so. The vast majority is not here, but yonder in the spirit-realm, and they, rather than the few millions now on earth, are the human race. It is we who are the fractional part, and are separated from our race, being but an inconsiderable minority, one fiftieth, perhaps only one one-hundredth of the whole. When we die we join the race, instead of separating from it. Think often of this, my hearer. You are now one of the children left behind by the family, who are congregated elsewhere. But you will soon join the more than one hundred thousand millions of fellow men who now inhabit the unseen land, of which the poet has said:

> " Earth has hosts, but thou canst show
> Many a million for her one;
> Through thy gates the mortal flow
> Has for countless years rolled on."
>
> *Croly.*

If this be true, what significant implications go with the fact! For these millions cannot be a mere idle, impassive, unorganized crowd of spirits, an aggregation of shadows. They are full of living activities. They carried with them thought, feeling and will. They have stores of knowledge, large and varied experience, definite character, wondrous powers of action, social natures, habits of organization, high aspirations, grand ambitions, capacities of exalted enjoyment. These qualities stand related to corresponding opportunities, and imply action, and, with such numbers and ages of time, imply action on a vast scale and for important ends. The next world must be a very busy as well as a very populous world, full of plans, efforts and results, so that life

there must be more rather than less real than it is
here. When a youth leaves the small circle under
the parental roof, or when a student quits the larger
circle of his schoolmates, and goes out into the busy
scenes of earth, to act his part in new relations, does
not his life take on added reality? So, my hearer,
will it be with you, when you shall emerge from
mortal childhood, and shall graduate from this
earthly school, and shall take your place with the
adult portion of the human race amid the settled
pursuits of eternity. Real life will then begin.

7.—And now, *apply the principle before recommended, of bringing the general down to the particular,
and picture to yourself the individual persons whom
you know to have entered upon the next life.* Follow
them there, and imagine them pursuing some active
course of life correspondent with their earthly pursuits; engaged in observation and reflection, in
study and effort, in individual enterprises and in
coöperative labors, developing and applying the
powers which they displayed here below. Do not
think of a nameless crowd of good men dwelling
there, but of particular persons of whom you have
read and in whose experience you have been interested. Say to yourself, there are the early saints;
Abel and Enoch and Noah; also Abraham and
Moses and David; Elijah and Isaiah and Daniel.
There, too, are the New Testament worthies, Simeon
and Anna; Mary and John the Baptist; Peter and
John and Paul. There are Clemens, Polycarp and

Augustine; Luther, Calvin and Knox; Wesley,
Whitfield and Edwards; Brainard, Martyn and
Livingstone; and the other grand, good men, whose
names are dear to us as the friends of God and man
during their earthly pilgrimage. They are still at
work for the Master, in appointed modes of service,
more busy and loving and helpful than ever. Come
still closer to yourself, my hearer, and picture in
that most real world the forms of those whom you
have personally known and loved. You remember
the exact image of that departed husband or wife,
parent or child, brother or sister, Christian friend or
beloved pastor. Bring up to memory all these dear
ones, in the undying part of their nature; in their
clearness of thought, in their vigor of reasoning, in
their soundness of judgment, in their breadth of
sympathy, in their wealth of affection, in their force
of will, in their practical efficiency. How real these
personal qualities were. How sensibly they affected you every day and constituted the real selves
of those whom you so dearly loved in the bye-gone
times. Think, then, not of their former bodily organization, and thus of their lying insensible in the
grave; but always conceive of their spiritual nature,
their true selves, which could not die. Then you will
always imagine them as now living and as acting
with increased powers. Name them over, in thought
and often in word, as those who are actually in full
and blessed employment in that world of life to
which they have gone. If, like myself, you have

reached old age, these departed friends are very numerous; if assembled, they would fill an immense audience room. Would it not seem quite natural, should you, some day, step into a church, and see them sitting there, as of old, with their familiar faces and pleasant expressions? That is much as it will be, when some day you step into heaven, and find them all there. Ah, how real the very thought of this makes heaven seem! So Whittier sings:

> " I have friends in spirit-land ;
> Not shadows in a shadowy band ;
> Not others, but themselves are they.
> And still I think of them the same
> As when the Master's summons came ;
> Their change, the holy morn-light breaking
> Upon the dream-worn sleeper, waking,
> A change from twilight into day."

8.—Shall I suggest one other method of making the next life seem real ; of making heaven approach visibility? It shall be that of *the study of the death-bed scenes of Christian believers*, whereby you may learn how much sense of reality they had, as they passed out of the present life into the next. Consult the many memoirs of departed saints, and recall scenes of which you may have been an eye-witness. There was bodily weakness, indeed, but accompanied by what marvelous spiritual strength and clearness of vision, as if of a present reality. You remember how Payson, on his dying bed exclaimed: " The celestial city is full in my view.

Its glories beam upon me, its breezes fan me, its odors are wafted to me, its sounds strike upon my ears, and its spirit is breathed into my heart. Nothing separates me from it, but the river of death, which now appears but as an insignificant rill, that may be crossed at a single step, whenever God shall give permission." Again he said: " My soul, instead of growing weaker and more languishing, as my body does, seems to be endued with an angel's energies, and to be ready to break from the body and join those around the throne." " It seems as if my soul had found a pair of new wings and was so eager to try them, that in her fluttering she would rend the fine net work of the body to pieces."

Sometimes the reality bursts for an instant on earthly vision, as in a case of an eminently godly woman of whose dying experience I was recently told by a minister. She was his wife's mother, and the family were plain, unimaginative farmer-folk. As, at the last moment, they stood around the bed, they repeated comforting passages of Scripture. It was a clear and cloudless day, just at noon. Suddenly the apartment was filled with a radiance beyond that of the sunlight, and so insufferably bright, that it could not be endured but for an instant. As the spectators looked at the aged dying saint, great was their amazement to see, in her place, amid the unearthly glory, the beauteous form of a *young* woman ; as if, at that moment, the glorified body had emerged from the decaying earthy tabernacle. They all saw the same unexpected sight, and they found that the breath had fled from the body. This glimpse of the coming life had the stamp of the actual. I have no time to cite other illustrations, which would easily occupy hours. The point is not, to exhibit the happiness, which faith in Christ can substitute for the ordinary fear of death, but to draw attention to the sense of reality, as regards the world to come, which then oftentimes floods the soul, reminding one of the martyred Stephen, who "being full of the Holy Ghost, looked up steadfastly into heaven and saw the glory of God, and Jesus standing on the right hand of God," and whose last words were, "Lord Jesus receive my spirit." I am sorry that it is not the fashion to be interested in Christian memoirs. They wonderfully strengthen faith, and brighten hope, and whoever makes himself familiar with the dying testimonies which they record, and calls often to mind the particulars of the exit of eminent believers from the world, will find the next life to be a growing reality to his mind, while the parting veil will become so thin as to be well nigh transparent.

The effect of this state of mind is described in the text : "If we hope for that we see not, then do we with patience wait for it." Present cares and trials weigh lightly upon one who lives much in the future, while they often crush him who is engrossed in the passing moment. Patience is born of hope, and the clearer our vision of the future, the greater is our power of endurance amid temporary ills.

> " In your patience ye are strong ; cold and heat ye take not wrong ;
> When the trumpet of the angel blows eternity's evangel,
>   Time will seem to you not long."

So Paul reasoned, in another epistle, when he wrote : " For our light affliction, which is but for a moment worketh for us a far more exceeding and eternal weight of glory, while we look not at the things which are seen, but at the things which are not seen : for the things which are seen are temporal ; but the things which are not seen are eternal."

And then, when the end of earth shall come, we shall not (as the dying skeptic called it) "take a leap in the dark," but amid the radiance bursting in shall wing our way to glory. We shall not seem to be leaving reality behind us, but to be retiring from shadows, and advancing into the only real state of being.